D1335982

To Vineeta
D.M.

First published in 2022 by Nosy Crow Ltd

The Crow's Nest, 14 Baden Place

Crosby Row, London, SE1 1YW, UK

Nosy Crow Eireann Ltd

44 Orchard Grove, Kenmare

Co Kerry, V93 FY22, Ireland

www.nosycrow.com

ISBN 978 1 78800 992 8 (HB)

ISBN 978 1 78800 993 5 (PB)

A CIP catalogue record for this book is available from the British Library.

Printed in China

Papers used by Nosy Crow are made from wood grown in sustainable forests.

10 9 8 7 6 5 4 3 2 1 (HB)

10 9 8 7 6 5 4 3 2 1 (PB)

Ruffles

and the **new green thing**

David Melling

This is **Ruffles.**

Ruffles **loves** . . .

singing . . .

scratching . . .

eating . . .

fetching . . .

sniffing . . .

chewing . . .

digging . . .

running . . .

and sleeping.

Ruffles **does not love** the new green thing.

And the **new green** thing is sitting in his bowl.

Ruffles has never seen anything like it before.

New. And green. And sitting in his bowl.

What **is** it?

Ruffles thinks . . .   and creeps . . .   and stares . . .

and listens . . .   and circles . . .   and pokes . . .

and sits . . .   and smells . . .   and thinks again.

But look! Ralph has come to play.

Ralph always digs the **deepest** holes . . .

Ralph always finds the **biggest** sticks . . .

And Ralph always jumps the **highest** fences.

And they **both** love to . . .

tug . . .   and scratch . . .   and play . . .

and run . . .   and race . . .   and chase . . .

and howl . . .   and leap . . .   and sleep.

The **new green** thing is still in Ruffles' bowl . . .

Ralph looks at it. And takes a **big** bite.

Gulp!

Well! If Ralph can try the **new green** thing . . .

then Ruffles can too!

He nibbles . . .

and gnaws . . .

and chews . . .

and munches . . .

and crunches . . .

and chomps . . .

and gobbles . . .

and guzzles . . .

and gulps until . . .

the **new green** thing is **all gone.**

And it was . . .

delicio

us!

Ruffles **loves** . . .

singing . . .

scratching . . .

eating . . .

fetching . . .

sniffing . . .

chewing . . .

digging . . .

running . . .

and Ralph.

But most of all, Ruffles **loves** new things . . .

Unless they're orange.